THE LITTLE MERMAID

The Little Mermaid
Retold and Illustrated by Fred Crump, Jr.
Based upon The Little Mermaid, *a fairy tale by Hans Christian Andersen*

Published by UMI (Urban Ministries, Inc.)
Chicago, Illinois

Text and illustrations copyright © 2007 by UMI (Urban Ministries, Inc.)

Copyright © 2007 UMI (Urban Ministries, Inc.).

Library of Congress Control Number: 2007904190

Hardcover Library of Congress Control Number: 2007904410

ISBN 10: 1-60352-063-5
HARDCOVER ISBN 10: 1-934056-72-3
ISBN 13: 978-1-60352-063-8
HARDCOVER ISBN 13: 978-1-934056-72-1

Produced by Color-Bridge Books, LLC
Printed in the U.S.A.

The Little Mermaid

Retold and Illustrated by
Fred Crump, Jr.

Urban Ministries, Inc.

ong ago and far away, in a water kingdom of coral and pearls, there lived a little mermaid. Her name was Ondina, and she was a princess of the sea. Her father, King Neptha, gave his beloved daughter any treasure she desired. All he asked in return was to hear her melodious voice every day. However, the one thing she wanted most was not in his power to give.

When she was younger, Ondina loved the wonders of her water world. But as she grew older, she discovered there was another world above the water. More than anything else, she wished to have legs instead of a fish tail so that she might walk among the land people. This was the one wish that her father could not grant.

Ondina, the Little Mermaid

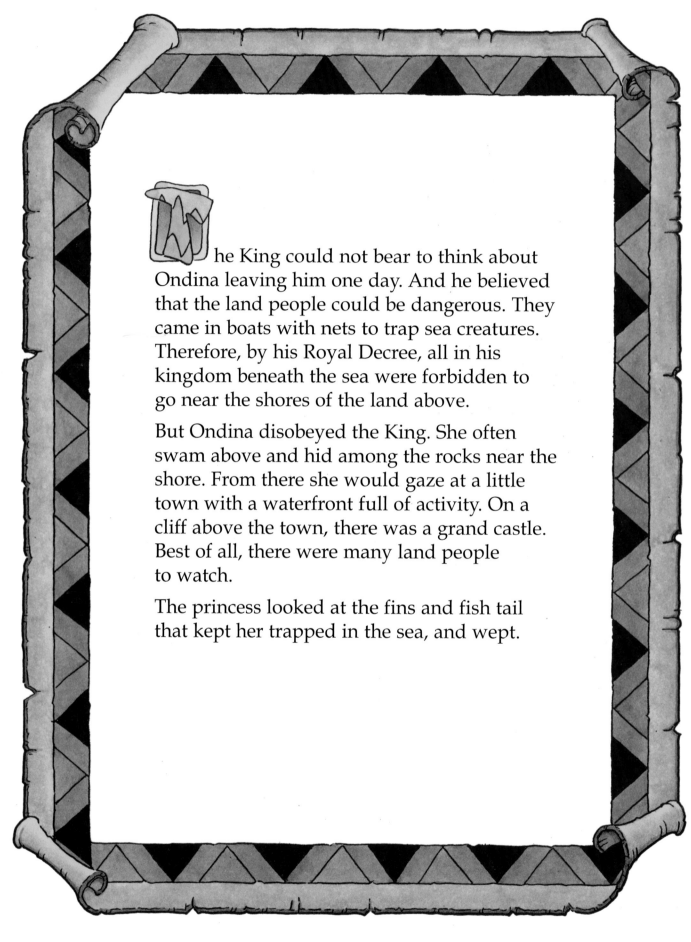

he King could not bear to think about Ondina leaving him one day. And he believed that the land people could be dangerous. They came in boats with nets to trap sea creatures. Therefore, by his Royal Decree, all in his kingdom beneath the sea were forbidden to go near the shores of the land above.

But Ondina disobeyed the King. She often swam above and hid among the rocks near the shore. From there she would gaze at a little town with a waterfront full of activity. On a cliff above the town, there was a grand castle. Best of all, there were many land people to watch.

The princess looked at the fins and fish tail that kept her trapped in the sea, and wept.

Ondina longed to live on land

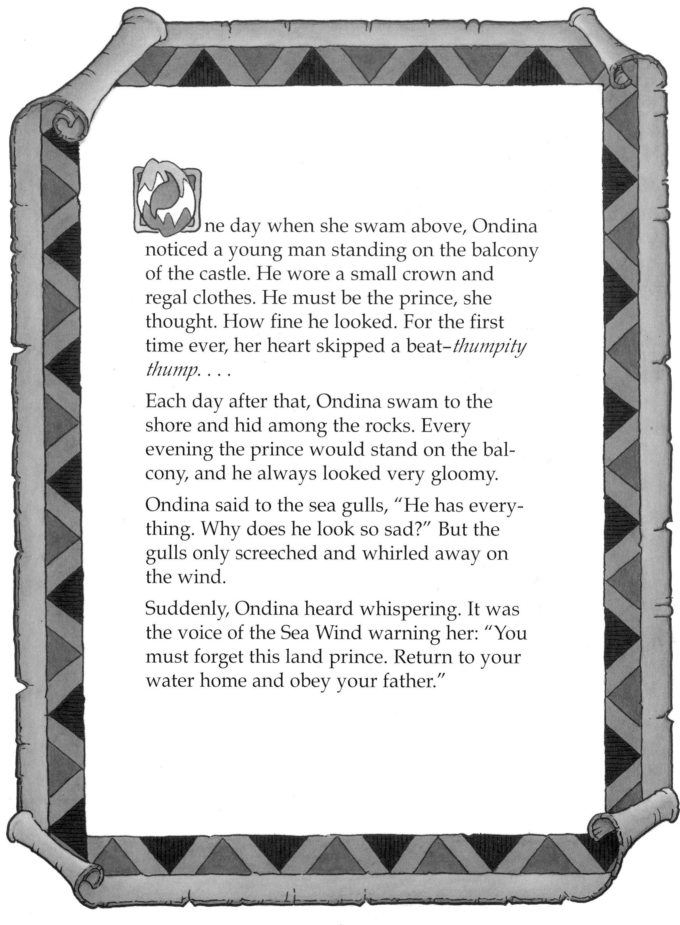

One day when she swam above, Ondina noticed a young man standing on the balcony of the castle. He wore a small crown and regal clothes. He must be the prince, she thought. How fine he looked. For the first time ever, her heart skipped a beat–*thumpity thump.* . . .

Each day after that, Ondina swam to the shore and hid among the rocks. Every evening the prince would stand on the balcony, and he always looked very gloomy.

Ondina said to the sea gulls, "He has everything. Why does he look so sad?" But the gulls only screeched and whirled away on the wind.

Suddenly, Ondina heard whispering. It was the voice of the Sea Wind warning her: "You must forget this land prince. Return to your water home and obey your father."

She saw the Prince

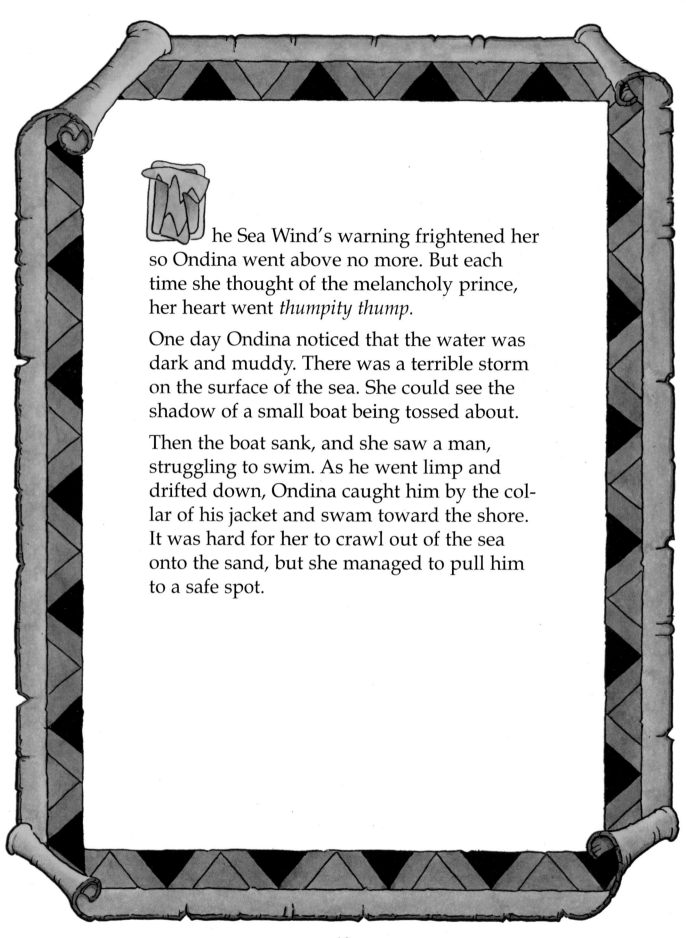

he Sea Wind's warning frightened her so Ondina went above no more. But each time she thought of the melancholy prince, her heart went *thumpity thump.*

One day Ondina noticed that the water was dark and muddy. There was a terrible storm on the surface of the sea. She could see the shadow of a small boat being tossed about.

Then the boat sank, and she saw a man, struggling to swim. As he went limp and drifted down, Ondina caught him by the collar of his jacket and swam toward the shore. It was hard for her to crawl out of the sea onto the sand, but she managed to pull him to a safe spot.

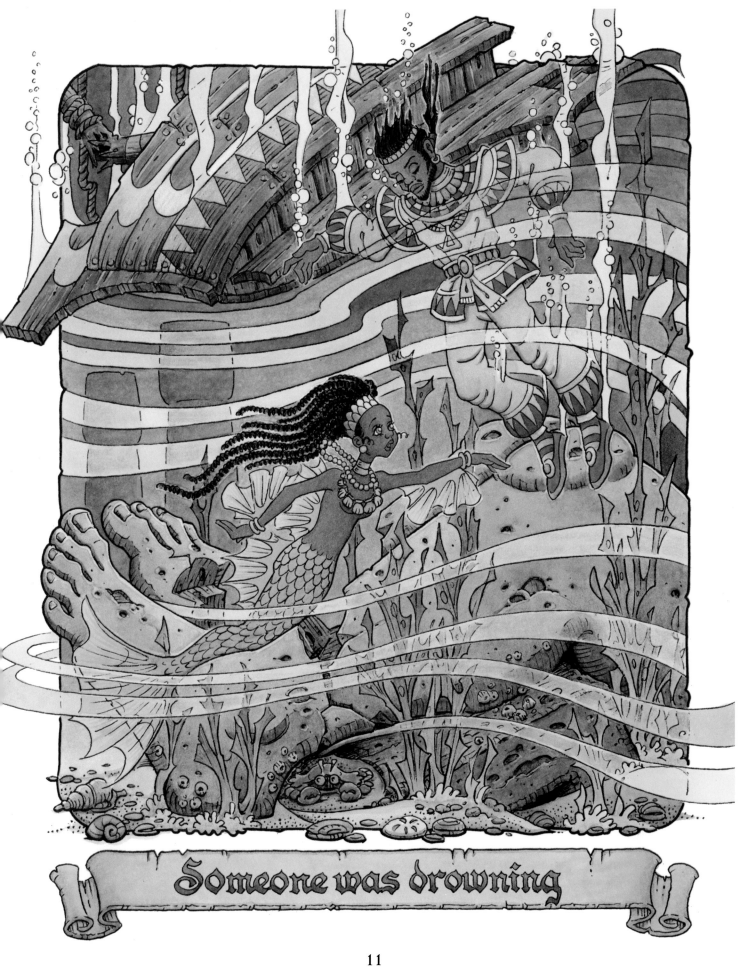

Someone was drowning

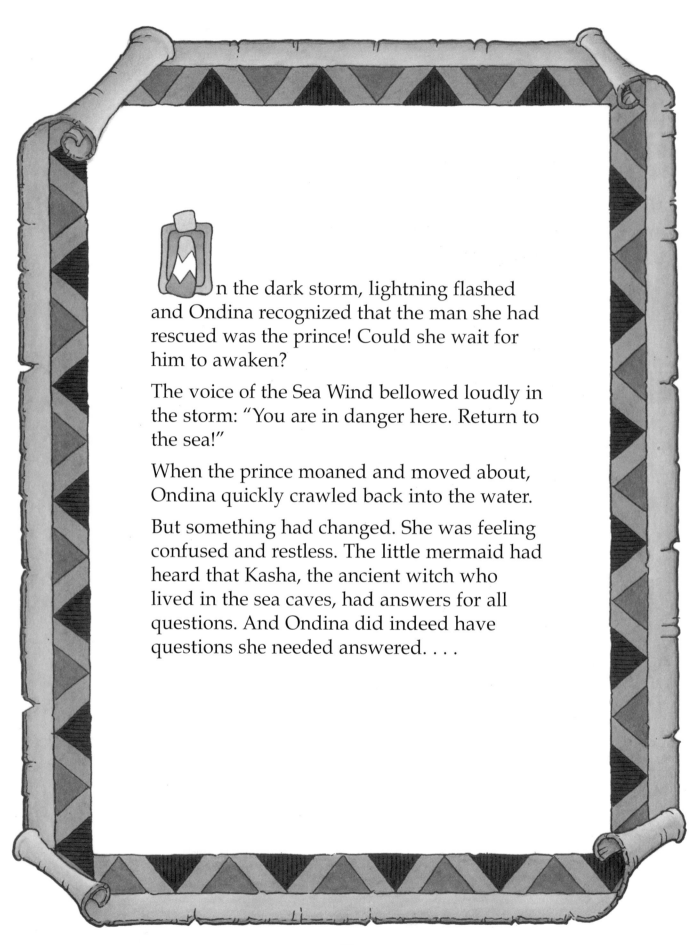

In the dark storm, lightning flashed and Ondina recognized that the man she had rescued was the prince! Could she wait for him to awaken?

The voice of the Sea Wind bellowed loudly in the storm: "You are in danger here. Return to the sea!"

When the prince moaned and moved about, Ondina quickly crawled back into the water.

But something had changed. She was feeling confused and restless. The little mermaid had heard that Kasha, the ancient witch who lived in the sea caves, had answers for all questions. And Ondina did indeed have questions she needed answered. . . .

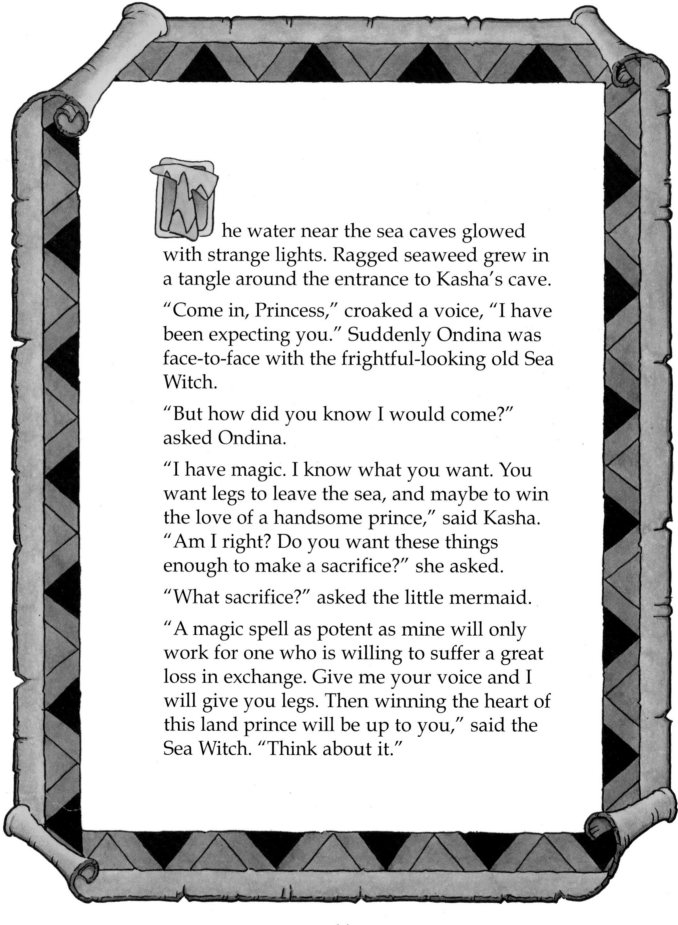

he water near the sea caves glowed with strange lights. Ragged seaweed grew in a tangle around the entrance to Kasha's cave.

"Come in, Princess," croaked a voice, "I have been expecting you." Suddenly Ondina was face-to-face with the frightful-looking old Sea Witch.

"But how did you know I would come?" asked Ondina.

"I have magic. I know what you want. You want legs to leave the sea, and maybe to win the love of a handsome prince," said Kasha. "Am I right? Do you want these things enough to make a sacrifice?" she asked.

"What sacrifice?" asked the little mermaid.

"A magic spell as potent as mine will only work for one who is willing to suffer a great loss in exchange. Give me your voice and I will give you legs. Then winning the heart of this land prince will be up to you," said the Sea Witch. "Think about it."

The Sea Witch

er voice? Could the little mermaid give up the voice her father loved so well?

For three days, Ondina swam restlessly around the water kingdom, making King Neptha very anxious. On the third day, she swam to the forbidden shore. She saw that the prince had recovered and was standing on his balcony. Her thumpity heart let her know what choice she would make.

She went one last time to see her sad father, and hoped for the right words to say. She could think of nothing that sounded right, but the wise old sea king knew. The little mermaid's childhood was over, and she was leaving his protection.

She was on her own now.

The Silent Farewell

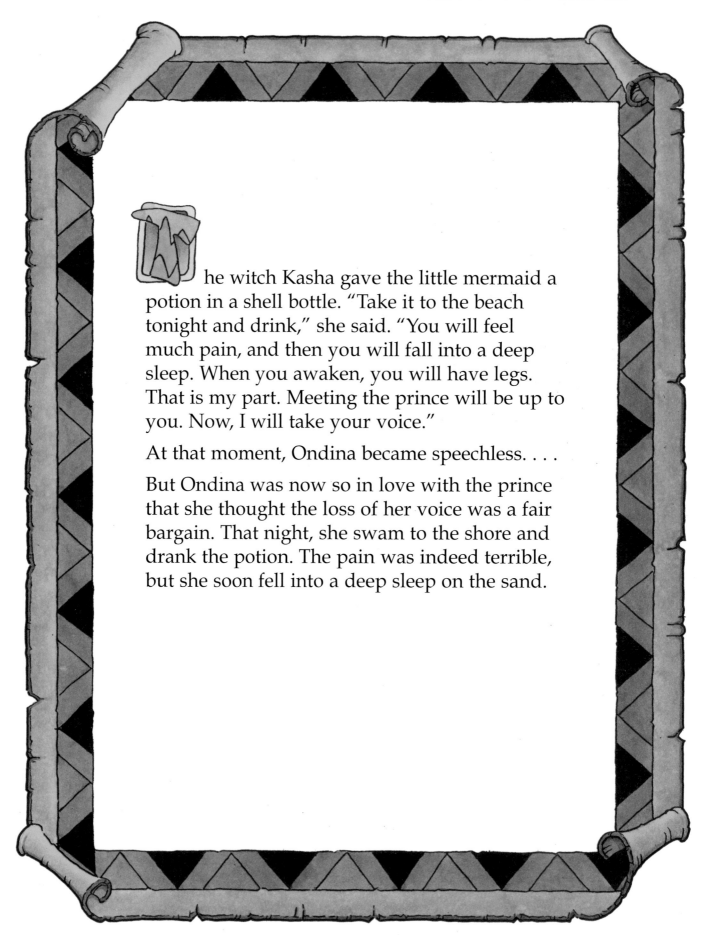

he witch Kasha gave the little mermaid a potion in a shell bottle. "Take it to the beach tonight and drink," she said. "You will feel much pain, and then you will fall into a deep sleep. When you awaken, you will have legs. That is my part. Meeting the prince will be up to you. Now, I will take your voice."

At that moment, Ondina became speechless. . . .

But Ondina was now so in love with the prince that she thought the loss of her voice was a fair bargain. That night, she swam to the shore and drank the potion. The pain was indeed terrible, but she soon fell into a deep sleep on the sand.

Ondina drank the Potion

hen Ondina awoke, she was in a soft, cozy bed inside the castle, and she was wearing strange clothes. When she moved, she saw that her fins were gone and her fish tail had become two strong legs.

She leaped out of the bed and was able to walk with grace and poise. Her wish had come true!

Servants came to attend her and were puzzled to discover she could not speak. They told her that fishermen had found her asleep on the sand. Everyone believed she had survived a shipwreck in the recent storm.

Ondina could only smile and nod and point. The servants dressed her in a beautiful gown and jeweled sandals. Then she was taken to meet the king and queen in the royal court.

The Wish came true

he servants whispered to the royal couple that the young lady was mute. Ondina curtsied and bowed her head, wishing she had a voice to greet them properly.

"Welcome, my dear," said the king. "We hope the memory of your shipwreck ordeal can be eased with us."

The queen said, "Until you are able to tell us where you belong, you may live here in the castle with our family."

And there was the prince—Ondina's reason for leaving the sea. The prince said, "I am Arak. Let me take you away from this stuffy court and give you a tour around the castle."

The prince gave her his hand and Ondina's heart went *thumpity thump,* over and over again.

Face to face at last

hen they finished looking around his palace home, the prince took Ondina to the balcony overlooking the sea.

"For weeks I have been waiting for something," he said, "and I have spent much time being gloomy out here. Now I think my wait is over."

Ondina wondered if he meant he was waiting for someone like her to come along. Was she to be the one?

"One day I was so grumpy and impatient, I foolishly went out to sea in a small boat during a storm," he said. "Probably the same storm that sank your ship also sank me. Then I dreamed a mermaid saved me, and I awoke safe on the shore."

If only Ondina could tell him it had not been a dream. But the next few days with Arak seemed to be worth the loss of her voice and her home in the sea.

He seemed more puzzled that she could neither read nor write. He told her about books, played music on his lute, and talked of strange lands and people. Ondina could only listen and enjoy the hours with him.

If only she could speak

hen one day she did not see him. Was he ill? she wondered. Was he on a trip? Or was he tired of being with her?

That evening, a servant came to escort her to the dining hall for a celebration. There sat the prince—with a beautiful young woman. When Prince Arak saw Ondina enter, he led her to the table.

"Anisia!" he said to the young woman. "This is the new little sister I told you about."

To Ondina he said, "Little silent sister, this is my future bride, for whom I've been waiting impatiently all these weeks."

Although Ondina felt faint, she managed to give Anisia a pleasant smile. In a daze, she joined them at the table. Arak and Anisia talked and laughed together, and held hands, and talked some more. But Ondina had to remain silent.

When she quietly slipped away, the merry couple did not even notice.

The Prince is to marry

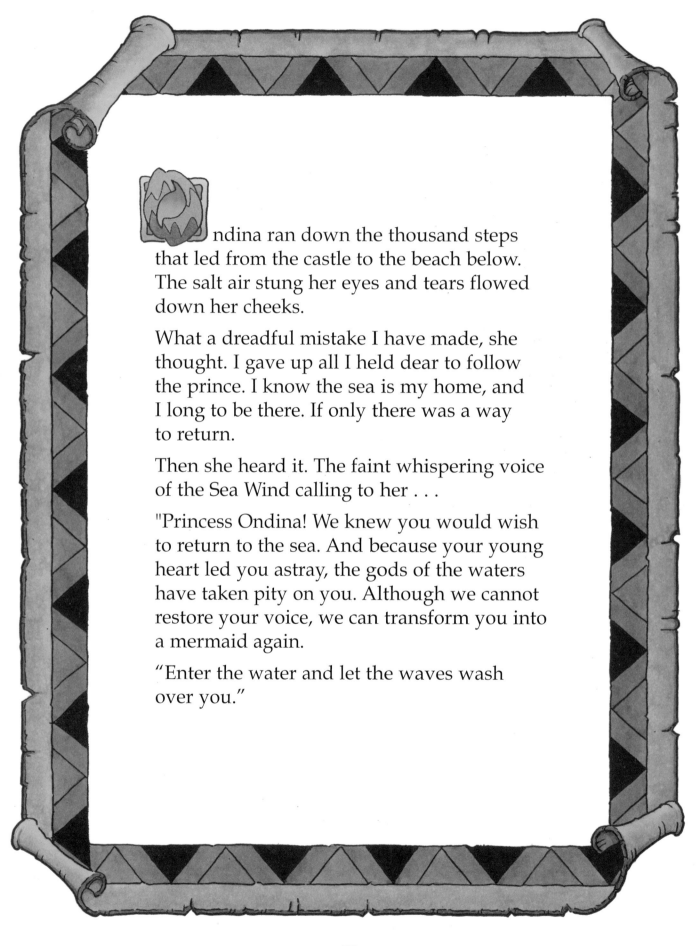

ndina ran down the thousand steps that led from the castle to the beach below. The salt air stung her eyes and tears flowed down her cheeks.

What a dreadful mistake I have made, she thought. I gave up all I held dear to follow the prince. I know the sea is my home, and I long to be there. If only there was a way to return.

Then she heard it. The faint whispering voice of the Sea Wind calling to her . . .

"Princess Ondina! We knew you would wish to return to the sea. And because your young heart led you astray, the gods of the waters have taken pity on you. Although we cannot restore your voice, we can transform you into a mermaid again.

"Enter the water and let the waves wash over you."

Is there any way?

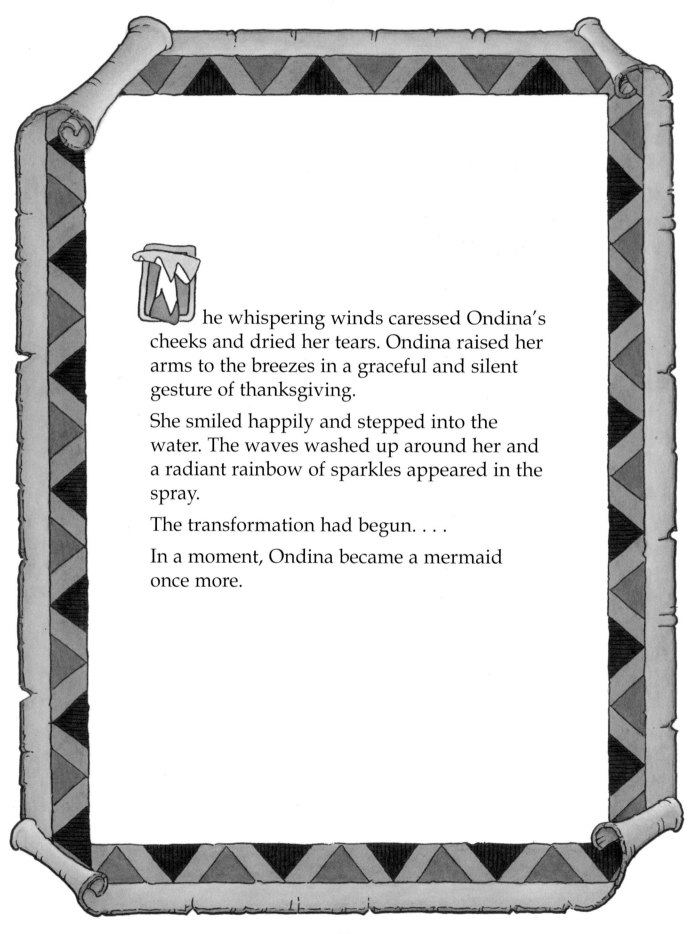

he whispering winds caressed Ondina's cheeks and dried her tears. Ondina raised her arms to the breezes in a graceful and silent gesture of thanksgiving.

She smiled happily and stepped into the water. The waves washed up around her and a radiant rainbow of sparkles appeared in the spray.

The transformation had begun. . . .

In a moment, Ondina became a mermaid once more.

Back to the sea

winkling foam and mist danced lightly on the waves in the moonlight. Deep below, Ondina swam excitedly back to her father and her beloved water kingdom of coral and pearls—speechless but happy to be back in the world where she belonged.

"Welcome home, Little Mermaid,"
whispered the Sea Wind.

32